My Robot Ate My Homework

Nancy Krulik and Amanda Burwasser

My Robot Ate My Homework

Illustrated by Mike Moran

Sky Pony Press
New York

First Edition

This is a work of fiction. Names, characters, places, and incidents are from the authors' imaginations, and used fictitiously.

Sky Pony Press books may be purchased in bulk at special discounts for sales promotion, corporate gifts, fund-raising, or educational purposes. Special editions can also be created to specifications. For details, contact the Special Sales Department, Sky Pony Press, 307 West 36th Street, 11th Floor, New York, NY 10018 or info@ skyhorsepublishing.com.

Sky Pony® is a registered trademark of Skyhorse Publishing, Inc.®, a Delaware corporation.

Visit our website at www.skyponypress.com.

Books, authors, and more at www.skyponypressblog.com.

www.realnancykrulik.com
www.mikemoran.net

10 9 8 7 6 5 4 3 2 1

Library of Congress Cataloging-in-Publication Data available on file.

Cover illustration by Mike Moran
Cover design by Sammy Yuen

Paperback ISBN: 978-1-5107-1030-6
Ebook ISBN 978-1-5107-1025-2

Printed in Canada

Interior Design by Joshua Barnaby

For Jeff and Amy,

two of the smartest smarty-pants I know

—NK

For Alex, the smartest cookie in the jar

—AB

To Patty and Kevin north of the Tappan Zee

—MM

CONTENTS

1.

What's the Point?

"Where is my geography work sheet?" I shouted as I dug through the homework pages scattered all over the kitchen table.

"Here it is, Logan," my cousin, Java, said. He pulled a sheet of paper out from under my toast.

I wiped a big smear of butter off the work sheet. Then I wrote my name and the date at the top.

I read the first question out loud.
"What river runs near Columbus,
Georgia?"

I looked at the map.

"The Chattahoochee River!" Java
shouted out.

He didn't even give me a chance to
find the answer for myself.

"Don't be such a show-off, Java,"
I groaned. But I started to write the
answer on my sheet anyway. *C-h . . .*

"How do you spell 'Chattahoochee'?" I asked him.

Before Java could answer, my mother walked into the kitchen.

"Finish up your breakfast," she said. "The bus will be here any second."

"I need another minute, Mom," I told her. "I just have to finish my homework."

"Well, don't blame me if you miss the bus and have to *walk* to school," Mom said. She turned to Java. "Is *your* homework finished?"

"Yes," Java told her. "It is in the homework folder, which is in my backpack."

"I'm glad *one* of you finished your homework on time," Mom said. She gave me a look.

"Homework is easy for Java," I told Mom. "He's a robot."

"I know," Mom admitted.

Of course she knew. Mom was the one who built Java.

My mom is a scientist. She likes to build things.

So she built me a robot cousin.

His name is **J**acob **A**lexander **V**ictor **A**pplebaum. But I just call him Java.

Sometimes it's kind of cool having a robot cousin by my side. Before Java, I was the only kid in the house. It's nice to have someone around to play catch or just hang out with.

But there are other times when having Java around can be a real pain. Especially when he does things like get his homework done perfectly, and on time.

Which I never do.

The hardest part about having Java in the family is I can't tell anyone he isn't human. That's because he's part of my mom's secret project: **Project Droid**.

Which is the perfect name for it, because that's what Java is. An android.

You just charge him up and he becomes a walking, talking, normal, eight-year-old kid.

Well, *sort of.*

There are some things about Java that aren't exactly normal kid–like.

Like, for starters, he has a computer brain, which means he's even smarter than our teacher.

And he's built to be super strong.

And to run really, really fast.

He can even take his head off, spin it
around, and put it back on backwards.
Which is actually pretty hilarious—
as long as he doesn't do it in front of
anyone but Mom and me.

I looked back down at my work sheet and started read the next question. *What are the names of the seven continents?*

Yay! I knew that one.

I started filling in the blanks. *Africa. Antarctica. Asia. Australia—*

Crack.

Before I could finish listing the continents, my pencil snapped.

Grrr. I was never going to get my homework done now.

"There's no point," I grumbled angrily.

Java's eyes opened wide.

"I can do it!" he shouted.

Java grabbed the pencil from my hand.

He stuck it in his mouth.

Then he turned the pencil around and around with his hand, while he ground away at the wood with his sharp teeth.

A moment later, Java handed the sharpened pencil back to me.

"Now it has a point," he said. *That's what I mean about him not being a normal kid.*

"Thanks, Java," I said.

I took the pencil back and tried to finish my work sheet.

"I am happy to help you, Logan," Java told me. "Always."

2.

Spaghetti for Brains

"Who can tell me the name of the world's largest island?" my teacher, Miss Perriwinkle, asked our class during our social studies lesson later that morning.

I tried to sink down under my desk. I had absolutely no idea. I hadn't gotten that far in the chapter we were supposed to read for homework.

I couldn't let Miss Perriwinkle call on me.

What would I say if she did? "My dog ate my homework"?

That would never work. I didn't have a dog.

All I had was a robot cousin. And I couldn't say my robot ate my homework.

For one thing, I didn't want anyone to know Java was a robot.

And for another, robots don't eat.

Jerry and Sherry Silverspoon raised their hands. But before Miss Perriwinkle could call on either of them—

"Greenland!" Java shouted out.

"That's correct, Java," Miss Perriwinkle told him. "But please raise your hand next time. Now, who can name the largest country in the world?"

Jerry raised his hand and said, "That's easy. China."

"No Jerry, *Russia* is the largest country in the world," Java corrected him. "China just has the most people."

"Very good, Java," Miss Perriwinkle said. She looked down at her list of questions.

Jerry rolled his eyes and stuck his

tongue out at Java.

The Silverspoon twins hate being wrong.

I love it when they're wrong.

"Where is the highest point on Earth?" Miss Perriwinkle asked us.

Nadine raised her hand. "The Eiffel Tower in Paris?" she responded.

The twins snickered.

"Everyone knows that's not it," Sherry said. "The highest point on Earth is Mount Everest."

Nadine frowned and looked down at her shoes.

Those Silverspoons sure were mean.

But they were pretty smart, too.

"That's right," Miss Perriwinkle told

Sherry. "Does anyone know what country is shaped like a boot?"

The twins were really on a roll now. Their hands shot up quickly.

"Jerry," Miss Perriwinkle said, pointing at him.

"Italy," Jerry answered proudly.

"Correct," Miss Perriwinkle told him.

"I love Italy," Jerry said. "That's where pasta comes from. I really like spaghetti."

"Actually, pasta wasn't invented in Italy," Java told him. "Marco Polo was an Italian explorer. He brought spaghetti back to Italy from China."

Miss Perriwinkle gave Java a big, proud smile. "Correct," she said.

The twins did not look happy.

Which made me *really* happy.

Brrinng. Just then, the bell rang.

"Put your notebooks in your desks and line up for music class," Miss Perriwinkle told us.

As I got in line, Jerry and Sherry walked past me and giggled.

"I guess Java must have gotten all the brains in your family," Sherry sneered at me. "Because you sure didn't."

I frowned. Maybe Sherry was right.

Compared to Java, it did feel like I had spaghetti for brains.

3.

A One-Droid Band

"*Hot cross buns! Hot cross buns!*"

My whole class was singing in the music room.

Well, *almost* my whole class. I wasn't singing. I'm a really lousy singer.

"Stop! Stop!" our music teacher, Mr. Fluff, said. "Somebody missed a note. Stanley, why don't you show us how it's done?"

Stanley stood up straight.

He cleared his throat.

He looked up at the musical notes that were written on the board.

And then he began to sing. *"Hot cross buns! Hot cross buns! One a penny, two a penny, hot cross buns!"*

Wow! Stanley sounded like an opera singer.

Everybody was impressed.

Even the Silverspoons. I could tell by how angry they looked.

The twins were *always* angry when they couldn't figure out a way to make fun of someone.

Jerry raised his hand.

"Yes?" Mr. Fluff asked him.

"I think we should sing a different song," Jerry said.

"Oh really?" Mr. Fluff asked. "Which song would that be?"

"One Sherry and I have been practicing," Jerry answered.

"We wrote it ourselves," Sherry added proudly.

Oh brother.

"I'm sure your song is lovely," Mr. Fluff told the twins, "but today we are singing 'Hot Cross Buns.' It's a famous folk song. People have been singing it for hundreds of years."

"That's true," Java said. "It was written in London in 1798."

"London is the capital of England, right?" Stanley asked.

"Yes, it is," Mr. Fluff said. "I thought it would be nice to sing something from another country, since you are studying geography. Now—"

"But our song is so much better," Jerry interrupted. "It's about twins."

"Everyone loves twins," Sherry added.

Not everyone, I thought angrily.

"What's a hot cross bun anyway?" Sherry asked.

"There are a few definitions of buns," Java answered. "A bun is a type of sweet roll. It is also a hairstyle that ballerinas wear. And some humans use the word buns to refer to their rear end—"

All of us kids started laughing. Even the Silverspoons.

But Mr. Fluff wasn't laughing.

"Java!" Mr. Fluff scolded. "Rear ends are not something we talk about in music class. Now, please. Let's try singing again."

Everyone—but me—began singing. *"Hot cross buns! Hot cross buns! One a—"*

"Wait! Wait!" Mr. Fluff stopped us again. He looked straight at me. "Logan, why aren't you singing?"

"I'm sorry, Mr. Fluff," I said. "I just don't think I can hit that high note."

Java smiled. His eyes opened wide.

"I can do it!" he shouted.

"Java, no!" I yelled.

But I was too late.

My cousin ran up to the front of the room.

He jumped high in the air.

And he punched his fist right through the highest note Mr. Fluff had written on the board.

Everyone stared at him.

"That is how you hit a high note," Java announced to the class.

"Oh no!" Mr. Fluff shouted. "The principal is going to be so angry when he sees that!"

Java had a goofy smile on his face. He couldn't understand why anyone would be angry.

Java doesn't understand a lot of things.

Mr. Fluff ran out of the room to get the janitor.

We all just stood there. We didn't know what to do.

"Nice move, doofus," Jerry said. He slapped Java on the back.

Boom!

A loud drum sound echoed from the back of my cousin's body.

"Hey, how did you do that?" Jerry askcd, surprised.

"It is the way I am made," Java replied. "It sounds louder from my stomach."

Java began banging on his stomach. It sounded like a drum.

Boom. Boom. Boom.

"That's so cool," Nadine told him.

"No it's not," Sherry said. "It's weird."

Tweet, tweet. Flute sounds blew out of Java's nostrils.

Honk. Honk. When he flapped his arms, horn sounds came out of his pits.

This was bad. *Really bad.* I had to cover for him.

"*Hot cross buns!*" I sang loudly so maybe no one would hear him. "*Hot cross buns . . .*"

"*One a penny, two a penny,*" Stanley joined in with his opera voice.

"Hot cross buns!" Nadine sang out.

Soon everyone was singing along with the music Java was making.

The Silverspoons may have thought Java was weird for being a one-man band, but the other kids seemed to think it was pretty cool.

And no one was wondering how he was doing it.

Which was a good thing. Because I had no idea how to explain it to them—without telling everyone my cousin was actually an android.

Ring, ring. Java wiggled his ears. They sounded just like bells.

Twang, twang. He plucked the strands of his hair so they sounded like guitar strings.

Crash! Crash! He clapped his hands together so hard, they sounded like cymbals!

"*Hot cross buns*," we sang. "*Hot cross buns . . .*"

And then . . .

OOOOMPPPPAAAA! Suddenly, Java let out an explosive noise. It sounded like a tuba.

I don't want to say where that tuba noise exploded from.

It would be too embarrassing.

4.

Icky Sticky

"Math is so hard!" I shouted angrily later that day as I sat in my room staring at my homework sheet. "I'm going to be up all night doing this."

The math problems were really tough.

Even worse, I was getting a late start on my homework.

Mr. Fluff and Principal Kumquat had made Java stay after school to help the janitor fix the SMART Board in the music room.

I'd stayed after school with him—just to make sure he didn't do anything too android-like.

So in a way, this was all Java's fault. Which just made me madder.

"What is wrong, Logan?" Java asked me.

"It's this math homework." I threw my calculator across the room. "I'm pulling my hair out over it."

"I can do it!" Java shouted out suddenly. He reached over and yanked a hair from the back of my head.

"Ow!" I yelled. "What did you do that for?"

"I was helping you pull your hair out," Java told me. He held up a strand of my hair. "This one still has the root on it."

"I don't need your help," I said angrily. *Or did I. . . .*

I started to think. Maybe I *did* need Java's help. After all, he was the brains in the family. Wasn't that what the Silverspoon twins had said?

"Actually, Java, I was thinking you *could* help me with my homework," I said. "How about you do this math work sheet for me?"

"You want me to do your work for you?" Java asked. "Isn't that against rule two hundred forty-seven in the school handbook?"

Leave it to Java to have memorized the whole school handbook.

"I think it is against rule four hundred fifty-nine, too," Java said. "And also rule . . ."

Oh brother.

"Didn't you say you'd always be happy to help me?" I asked, interrupting him.

Java nodded. "Yes."

"Well, then you should help me now," I told him. "A real friend always sticks to his word."

Java jumped up from his chair. He opened my top desk drawer and grabbed a big bottle of paste.

"I can do it!" he shouted. He began to cover his face with icky, sticky paste.

"What are you doing?" I asked him.

Java reached into his backpack and grabbed one of his vocabulary flash cards. He slathered paste on the card and stuck it on to his forehead.

"I am sticking to my word," Java said. "The word on this card is *absorb*. It means to soak up."

I shook my head. "That's not what it means," I told him.

"I know I am correct, Logan," Java said. "My database has a state-of-the-art dictionary. *Absorb* means to soak up. It can also mean to take in."

"No. I meant that's not what *sticking to your word* means," I explained to my cousin. "It means keeping your promise. And you did sort of promise you would help me if I needed it."

Java was quiet for a moment. His eyes rolled around in his head. I figured his hard drive was trying to compute what I had just said.

"I will help you, Logan," Java told me finally.

"Terrific!" I handed my math book to Java. "Why don't you start with this? We have to do all the problems on pages seventeen and eighteen."

"Yes, Logan," he agreed.

My genius cousin went right to work doing my subtraction problems.

Meanwhile, I sat on my bed and practiced pulling a turtle out of my magic hat. That's no easy trick. It's almost as hard as math— at least for me.

But math isn't hard for Java.

"All finished!" he said a moment later.

"Great," I told him. "Now, here's my spelling homework." I handed him my spelling book.

Then I went outside to kick my soccer ball against the side of the house.

"All finished!" Java called to me from my window a few minutes later.

"Good job," I replied. "Now read the first three chapters in the history book."

"Okay, Logan," Java said.

He opened the book to chapter one.

I went inside and poured myself a big bowl of Sugar Teeth cereal.

Having Java help me was working out really well.

As soon as he finished reading the
history pages, Java started working on
my science work sheet.

While he labeled the parts of a
cockroach, I clipped my toenails.

Java got busy clicking around on my computer, looking for a current events article to write about.

So I got busy making paper airplanes and flying them out the window.

While Java did my geography homework, I stood on my head and counted backward from ten.

"All finished!" Java announced finally. "That is the end of your homework, Logan."

Just then, my mother walked by. I quickly flipped back over onto my feet. "How's the homework coming, boys?" Mom asked us.

"Great!" I told her as I put the last work sheet in my homework folder. "We're both already finished. And I learned so much."

It wasn't a *total* lie.

I had learned how to get an airplane to do a loop-the-loop in the air.

"I'm proud of you, Logan," Mom said. "You've really been working hard."

I smiled at her. It felt so nice to get a compliment from Mom.

Although, I did feel a little guilty.

But *just* a little.

5.

Cheater, Cheater

"Here's another A-plus for you, Logan," Miss Perriwinkle said as she handed back my homework sheet on Friday afternoon.

I proudly took the paper from her hand.

"Logan and Java were the only two who got all the geography questions right— even the one about the Canary Islands," Miss Perriwinkle announced to the class.

"I can't believe I got that one wrong," Stanley said. "I thought I knew everything about canaries."

"The Canary Islands are not named for birds, Stanley," Java told him. "They are named for *canaria*, which is the Latin word for dogs."

Sherry and Jerry looked at each other and rolled their eyes.

"What a show-off," Jerry said.

"A real know-it-all," Sherry added.

I tucked the A-plus geography sheet into my backpack, on top of my A-plus science homework, which was next to my A-plus vocabulary homework.

I'd been getting A-plus papers back all week. *Thanks to Java.*

I sat back and smiled.

But the Silverspoon twins weren't smiling. They were not happy that I was finally getting higher grades on my homework than they were.

The minute Miss Perriwinkle turned her back, Sherry Silverspoon stuck her tongue out at me and crossed her eyes.

I didn't care.

Even the Silverspoons couldn't make me feel bad today.

I was the King of the Classroom.

The Chairman of the Chalkboard.

The Prince of the Pencils.

And a regular old smarty-pants.

"Okay, boys and girls," Miss Perriwinkle said. "You better put on your geography thinking caps this weekend. Because on Monday, we're having a geography bee!"

"I don't have information about that kind of bee in my hard drive," Java said. "I know that honey bees fly at fifteen miles per hour. And that sweat bees—"

"Sweat bees?" Nadine interrupted him. "Those sound gross."

"Sweat bees are dark colored," Java explained.

"And they—"

Hard drive?

Sweat bees?

Uh-oh.

I had to stop Java from talking, before everyone figured out he wasn't like the rest of us.

But Sherry Silverspoon beat me to it.

"Stop showing off, Java," Sherry told him. "You learned all that from us."

"We taught him a lot of bee facts for the science fair," Jerry added.

I couldn't believe it.

The Silverspoons didn't care that Java was acting like a walking, talking encyclopedia.

They just wanted to take the credit for what he knew.

"A geography bee has nothing to do with insects," Miss Perriwinkle explained. "It's a contest."

"How does the contest work?" Nadine asked her.

"Everyone will line up in the front of the room," Miss Perriwinkle explained. "I will ask each of you a question. If you answer correctly, you will stay in line. If you answer incorrectly, you will sit down."

"It's kind of like a spelling bee," Stanley said.

"Yes," Miss Perriwinkle told him. "Except I will be asking you geography questions. The last person left standing will be the winner."

The Silverspoon twins gave each other a look. I think they were trying to figure out which one of them would be the last one standing.

Sherry raised her hand.

"Yes, Sherry?" Miss Perriwinkle asked her.

"What do we get if we win?" Sherry wondered.

"The winner will get a medal," Miss Perriwinkle answered.

"Not a trophy?" Jerry asked. "Because we like trophies."

"We have a lot of them," Sherry added.

"The winner gets a *medal*," Miss Perriwinkle repeated. She smiled at the rest of us. "This is going to be great. You'll get to show off everything you learned by doing your homework this week."

Gulp.

Uh-oh.

I hadn't actually learned *anything* doing my homework this week.

Java had learned it all. He was the one who had done his homework. And mine.

Which meant on Monday, everyone—including the Silverspoons—was going to know the truth.

I wasn't the King of the Classroom.

Or the Chairman of the Chalkboard.

Or the Prince of the Pencils.

I was a cheater.

Cheater, cheater, poodle eater.

There was no way I was going to get through the first round of a geography bee. I didn't know Kalamazoo from Timbuktu.

This was going to be bad. *Really* bad.

6.

Time's Up!

Oh my gosh. Oh my gosh. Oh my gosh.

As soon as I got home from school, I threw my backpack on the porch.

I started pacing nervously up and down the driveway.

Oh my gosh. Oh my gosh. Oh my gosh.

What was I going to do? By Monday morning, my life was going to be over.

I was going to be a laughingstock.

Make that a *grounded* laughingstock. Because Mom was going to be furious when she found out that I'd gotten Java to do my homework all week.

I looked over at my android cousin. He was happily lying on our front lawn, counting blades of grass—by twos.

"Seven thousand six hundred fifty-four," he said. "Seven thousand six hundred fifty-six. Seven thousand six hundred fifty-eight. Seven thousand . . ."

"How can you just be lying there, all calm?" I asked him. "Aren't you nervous about the geography bee?"

"Why would I be nervous?" Java asked me. "I have all the information in my hard drive."

Java was lucky. He had a super-duper, high-powered hard drive.

All I had was a regular old human brain.

Wait a minute . . .

A brain is sort of like a hard drive. It just doesn't have as many wires and buttons. So if I could input the geography facts into *my* hard drive, I might be able to get through the geography bee without making a fool of myself.

I scooped up my backpack and ran into the house at top speed.

I found my mom standing in the kitchen. "Hi, Logan," she said. "Do you want some milk and kiwi?"

I shook my head. "No thanks," I said. "Where do we keep that old globe Grandpa gave us?"

"In my lab, right between Java's battery charger and the cherry pie machine I made last year," Mom replied.

The cherry pie machine! Boy, did I hate that thing.

The machine had exploded in the middle of our second-grade bake sale. It turned Principal Kumquat into a big, red, cherry-flavored mess.

After that, I wasn't allowed to bring anything to bake sales anymore.

"Why do you need a globe?" Mom asked me.

"I don't have time to explain," I told her. "I have way too much studying to do."

The Atlantic Ocean is saltier than the Pacific Ocean, I wrote on a flashcard.

The only continent that doesn't have any snakes or reptiles is Antarctica, I wrote on another.

I put those cards on the top of my growing pile of note cards. Then I took another bite of my blueberry and tuna fish sandwich. It tasted disgusting. But I kept chewing.

Java had told me that blueberries and tuna are supposed to be good for your brain. And my brain needed all the help it could get.

Iceland is green. And Greenland is ice. I wrote on another flashcard.

Just then, Java walked into my room.

"Do you want to throw a ball around for a while, Logan?" he asked me.

"Are you kidding?" I answered. "I have too much studying to do. I can't find the time to play ball right now."

Java's eyes lit up. He smiled.

"I can do it!" he shouted.

Java raced out into the hall. He came back a minute later holding my mom's big old cuckoo clock.

"Here," he told me. "I found the time!"

Cuckoo. Cuckoo. Cuckoo. Cuckoo. The little bird in the clock popped out and announced the time.

I looked over at my robot cousin and frowned.

The clock wasn't the only thing that was cuckoo in my house.

7.

Is There a Zoo in Kalamazoo?

I thought I was going to pee in my pants.

That's how nervous I was as I waited for my turn to answer a question in the geography bee on Monday morning.

Stanley had already answered his question about where penguins lived correctly. I wasn't surprised that Stanley knew penguins lived near Antarctica.

There wasn't very much about birds he didn't know.

Now it was Jerry Silverspoon's turn. "In what city was the hamburger invented?" Miss Perriwinkle asked him.

Jerry smiled. "That's too easy," he bragged. "I know all about hamburgers.

I eat them every Fourth of July. Hamburgers are from Germany."

I started to laugh. "Germany's not a city," I told him. "It's a country. Hamburgers come from the city of Hamburg. Which is *in* Germany."

Jerry looked like he was about to cry. "That's what I meant," he said.

Miss Perriwinkle smiled kindly. "It's okay, Jerry," she told him. "Take a seat. You'll do better in the next geography bee."

Jerry looked really mad. But he sat down anyway.

Nadine was next.

"Where is the largest pyramid found?" Miss Perriwinkle asked her.

Nadine smiled. She looked like she

knew this one for sure.

"Egypt," she said.

Oops. That wasn't right.

"Sorry, Nadine," Miss Perriwinkle told her. "The correct answer is Mexico."

Nadine frowned. She headed back to her desk with her head down.

Now it was Java's turn.

"What country gets its name from a Native American word for 'large village'?" Miss Perriwinkle asked him.

Java didn't have to think. "Canada," he said, right away.

"That's right," Miss Perriwinkle told him.

And now, finally, it was my turn. This was it.

As Miss Perriwinkle looked through her list of questions, my knees begin to shake.

My teeth started chattering.

And huge butterflies started flying all around in my stomach.

It didn't help that Jerry Silverspoon was sitting right in front of me hissing, "Miss, miss, miss," under his breath.

"Did you say something, Jerry?" Miss Perriwinkle asked him.

"Um . . . I was just saying that *Miss Perriwinkle's* dress is very nice today," Jerry answered.

What a liar!

"Thank you, Jerry," Miss Perriwinkle replied. "But please keep quiet now. It is Logan's turn to answer a question."

Gulp.

"In what country can you find the world's largest castle?" my teacher asked me.

Hooray! This was an easy one. I had read about the castle last night while I was sitting in a bubble bath.

"It's the Malbork Castle in Poland," I said proudly.

"That is correct," Miss Perriwinkle replied.

Phew. One question down.

About an hour later, we were down to just three people in the geography bee: Sherry Silverspoon, Java, and me.

Miss Perriwinkle turned to Sherry. "Can you tell me where the first zoo in the United States was built?" she asked.

Before Sherry could answer, Jerry started cheering her on. "Come on, sister. You know this one. Show the Applebaum airheads just who's boss."

Sherry smiled. "Don't worry," she told her brother. "I've got this. The first US zoo was built in Kalamazoo."

"Ha! You're wrong!" I exclaimed.

"Am not," Sherry told me. "I am *never* wrong."

"You are this time," I insisted.

"Logan, be kind," Miss Perriwinkle scolded me.

Sherry gave me one of her *ha-ha* looks. Like she was laughing at me for getting in trouble, without actually laughing at me.

"But I'm afraid you *are* wrong, Sherry," Miss Perriwinkle said.

I gave Sherry one of my *ha-ha* looks right back.

"The first zoo in the United States was built in Philadelphia in 1876," Java told her. "There is no zoo in Kalamazoo."

"Show-off," Sherry snapped at him as she went back to her seat.

Now it was just my cousin and me left standing.

Applebaum verses Applebaum.

"It's your turn, Logan," Miss Perriwinkle told me. "What is the name of the longest river in the world?"

"That's easy," I said. "The Nile River. It's in Egypt."

"Very good," Miss Perriwinkle said. "Your turn, Java. What do we call openings in the Earth's surface that sometimes let ash, gas, and hot magma escape?"

"Volcanoes," Java answered.

"Correct!" Miss Perriwinkle said excitedly. She turned to me. "Logan, how much land is there at the North Pole?"

Huh? I didn't remember reading anything about the North Pole.

Little drops of sweat started to form under my nose. I scratched at my armpit nervously.

I bit
my lip
and tried
to access that
information in my
hard drive.
Except I didn't
have a hard drive. I
had a brain. And at the
moment, it felt completely empty.

"I-I-I don't know," I said finally.

"Java?" Miss Perriwinkle asked. "Do you
know the answer? If you do, you are the
winner. If not, both you and Logan will
have a chance to answer another question."

Java's eyes began to roll around in his
head. I knew that meant he was searching
through his database.

Was it possible he didn't know the answer either? Did I still have a chance to win?

Java scratched wildly at the top of his head.

He wiggled his ears.

And stuck out his tongue to lick his nose.

All at the same time.

Uh-oh. I'd never seen Java do that before.

Was he short-circuiting?

Or overheating?

I sure hoped not.

I didn't want my cousin to explode in front of everyone. Even if it meant I would win the geography bee.

Finally, Java said, "That is a trick question, Miss Perriwinkle. There is no land at the North Pole. It is all ice on top of seawater."

Miss Perriwinkle stood up and started clapping. "Congratulations, Java. You are the winner of the geography bee."

I just stood there. Java had beaten me . . . again.

It wasn't fair.

He had a big advantage—a hard drive with a fully loaded database. A mere human couldn't compete with that.

But, of course, I didn't say that. I *couldn't* say that. Not without giving away Java's secret.

So I just shook his hand and said, "Congratulations, cousin."

It was the right thing to do.

You don't need a hard drive to know that nobody likes a sore loser.

8.

Smart Parts

"Java, Java! Hooray! Yippee! He just won our geography bee!" A bunch of the kids in my class were cheering for Java as we ran out onto the playground for recess.

The Silverspoon twins were not cheering. They were angry. I could tell by the way they stormed over to Stanley and me.

"Your cousin cheated," Sherry told me. "There's no way anyone could do what he did."

Uh-oh. Had the Silverspoons figured out Java's secret?

It was possible. They *were* pretty smart.

"I didn't see Java cheating," Stanley said. "He didn't have any notes written on his hands or his shoes or anything."

"I don't know how he did it," Sherry admitted. "But he must have. Otherwise he couldn't have beaten us."

Phew. The Silverspoons didn't know Java's secret after all.

"Nobody *ever* beats us," Jerry insisted.

"Until now," I said.

Jerry and Sherry didn't answer. They just stared at me.

Then they turned and stormed away.

Wow. The Silverspoons were speechless. I'd never seen them like that before.

It kind of made me feel like a winner, too.

"Is there anything your cousin can't do?" Stanley asked me. "First, he's a math master. Then he's a soccer star. And now he's the general of geography."

"Yeah, he's pretty amazing," I said.

"You did really well, too," Stanley told me. "I had no idea you knew so much about geography."

Stanley was right. I did know a lot about geography—now. And no one had programmed all that information into my head. I had learned it all by myself.

Java pushed his way through his crowd of cheering fans. He started walking over toward Stanley and me.

Nadine hurried to catch up with him.

"Looks like Nadine's heading this way," Stanley whispered to me.

"I see her. I see her," I whispered back. I ran my fingers through my hair and straightened my shirt. "H-h-hi, Nadine," I stammered.

Why do I always get so nervous when I see Nadine?

My cousin patted me stiffly on the back. "Excellent job, Logan," he told me. "You know a lot of geography."

"Yeah. But today you knew more." I pointed to the gold-colored medal around his neck.

"You guys were both bursting with brains," Nadine told Java and me.

"Thank you," Java said.

"Th-th-thanks, Nadine," I added nervously.

"I keep picturing how mad the Silverspoons looked when Java won that medal," Stanley said with a laugh.

"I can do it!" Java shouted out suddenly.

He reached into his backpack and pulled out a notebook and crayons.

Then he started drawing. I'd never seen anyone's fingers move that fast.

"What are you doing?" Stanley asked him.

"Picturing the Silverspoons," Java answered. He held up his notebook. "See? Here they are. In a picture."

I shook my head. Sometimes Java was so clueless.

But Nadine didn't think so.

"That's awesome!" she complimented my cousin. "Maybe you can draw a picture of *me* some time. Do you want to have a playdate after school? Are you free?"

"No," Java told her.

What? Stanley and I both stared at Java with surprise.

Nobody turned down a playdate with Nadine Vardez. Ever.

"I am not free," Java told her. "The combined cost of my parts is seventy-three thousand, eight hundred sixty-two dollars, and forty-seven cents."

Stanley and Nadine stared at him.
They looked very confused.

Not that I blamed them.
I had to do something. And fast.

"Hahaha," I laughed, pretending Java was making a joke. "Speaking of body parts, did you guys know that more than half of a human body is made up of water?"

Now Stanley and Nadine were staring at *me*. They had no idea why I had said that.

I wasn't really sure, either. It had just popped out.

"That is correct, Logan," Java told me.

"How did you know that?" Stanley asked me.

I had no idea.

"I must have read it somewhere," I told him.

"You're full of interesting information today, Logan," Nadine told me.

I felt my face start to sweat again. "Th-th-thanks," I stammered.

"Maybe the four of us can hang out together after school," Stanley said. "We can practice our soccer drills."

"That's a great idea, Stanley," Nadine told him.

"Yeah, it is," I said.

"There are thirty-two panels on a soccer ball," Java told us suddenly. "Soccer was played in ancient Egypt, ancient Rome, and ancient China."

"Is there anything you don't know, Java?" Nadine asked him.

"No," Java answered her. "There is not."

But I knew that wasn't true.

Sure, Java's electrical parts gave him plenty of smarts. But there were still lots of things he didn't understand.

Like what it meant to be free after school.

Or to hit a high note.

Or to stick to his word.

Or that no one says no to a playdate with Nadine Vardez.

Those were the kinds of things only a real human kid could understand.

As long as Java was my android cousin, I knew it was my job was to teach him everything I could about being human.

Because when it came to knowing how to get along with people, *I* was the Applebaum kid with all the smarts.

Use Your Noodle!

Logan sure showed those Silverspoon twins who had spaghetti for brains—and it wasn't Logan! He and Java beat Jerry and Sherry fair and square.

Java and Logan are geography geniuses. Thanks to them, the whole class now knows that noodles originally came from China, not Italy.

Here's a recipe for Chinese sesame noodles that's so easy it will have you shouting, "**I can do it!**" in no time. *(But don't do it alone. Make sure you have a grown-up with you to deal with the slicing, dicing, and boiling water.)*

Here's what you'll need:

 12 ounces thin noodles

 ¼ cup soy sauce

 ¼ cup canola oil

 3 tablespoons sesame oil

 2 tablespoons sugar

 2 tablespoons rice vinegar

 ½ teaspoon chili oil

 4 cloves of garlic, minced (You can also use two teaspoons of already minced garlic from a jar.)

 4 green onions/scallions, thinly sliced

 1 helpful grown-up cooking assistant

Adult

Sugar

Noodles

Rice Vinegar

Soy Sauce

Chili Oil

Canola Oil

Garlic

Sesame Oil

Scallions

Here's what you do:

 1 Ask a grown-up to bring a pot of water to a boil.

 2 Pour the noodles into the boiling water and cook them according to the directions on the package.

3 While the noodles are cooking, use a whisk to mix the soy sauce, canola oil, sesame oil, sugar, vinegar, chili oil, and garlic in a large bowl.

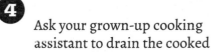

4 Ask your grown-up cooking assistant to drain the cooked noodles.

5 Pour the sauce over the cooked noodles. Then toss the noodles around in the sauce until all the noodles are evenly coated.

Sprinkle the onions over the noodles and serve them to your family and friends. There's plenty to go around. This recipe makes eight servings!

About the Authors

Nancy Krulik is the author of more than two hundred books for children and young adults including three *New York Times* bestsellers and the popular Katie Kazoo, Switcheroo; George Brown, Class Clown; and Magic Bone series. She lives in New York City with her husband and crazy beagle mix. Vist her online at www.realnancykrulik.com

Amanda Burwasser holds a BFA with honors in creative writing from Pratt Institute in New York City. Her senior thesis earned her the coveted Pratt Circle Award. A preschool teacher, she resides in Forestville, California.

About the Illustrator

Mike Moran is a dad, husband, and illustrator. His illustrations can be seen in children's books, animation, magazines, games, World Series programs, and more. He lives in Florham Park, New Jersey. Visit him online at www.mikemoran.net